*You do not need to read this page – just get on with the book!*

First published in 2009 in Great Britain by
Barrington Stoke Ltd
18 Walker St, Edinburgh, EH3 7LP

www.barringtonstoke.co.uk

ISBN: 978-1-84299-709-3

Printed in Great Britain by Bell & Bain Ltd

# AUTHOR ID

**Name:** Eric Brown

**Likes:** Time-travel and chocolate.

**Dislikes:** Being chased by dinosaurs.

**3 words that best describe me:**
I love books!

**A secret not many people know:**
I keep a space-ship at the bottom of the garden.

# ILLUSTRATOR ID

**Name:** Shona Grant

**Likes:** Gardening, walking along empty Scottish island beaches, chocolate.

**Dislikes:** Prunes and spiders.

**3 words that best describe me:**
Cheery animal lover.

**A secret not many people know:**
I'm 48 ... shhhhh!

To Freya

# Contents

# Chapter 1
# Dinosaur Home-work

It all began on Friday afternoon. I was walking home from school with my best friend Millie.

I said, "Mr Brooke gave us a lot of home-work. It'll take all weekend to do!"

"But it will be good fun," Millie said. "I love reading about dinosaurs."

I shook my head. "I think dinosaurs are boring," I said.

Millie smiled. "You are odd, Mouse! You must be the only boy in school who thinks dinosaurs are boring!"

Our teacher Mr Brooke loved to talk about dinosaurs. "Did you know," he had said today, "that some meat-eating dinosaurs had a great sense of smell? Also, did you know that no one knows what colour dinosaurs were?"

Now Millie said, "I've got lots of books about dinosaurs. Come round to my house and I'll help you with the home-work. It'll be fun!"

"But why do we need to know all that stuff about dinosaurs?" I said. "They died millions of years ago, so what's the point? We'll never meet any dinosaurs, will we?"

Millie just looked at me. "Mouse, it's fun to learn about things."

"Hey," I said. "What's that?"

A roar came from the sky.

"It sounds like ..." Millie began.

"But it can't be!" I said.

The roar grew louder. We put our hands over our ears.

Millie pointed. "Look, Mouse!"

A big silver space-ship landed in the field near the lane.

"It's Umba-Wumba's space-ship!" Millie said. "The one that's also a time-machine."

We jumped over a gate and ran to the space-time ship. I felt very happy because

soon I would see my good friend, the alien Umba-Wumba again.

Last year a space-ship grabbed Millie and me and took us to another planet. We met Umba-Wumba, and he helped us get away from the planet and fly back home.

He had said he would come to visit us again, and here he was.

A door in the side of the space-ship opened. Umba-Wumba ran out. He was round and orange, with four arms. He had an eye on the end of his long nose.

"Mouse and Millie!" he shouted. "It's great to see you again."

"Umba-Wumba!" we said.

We ran across the field and hugged our alien friend.

# Chapter 2
# A Great Idea

"Why are you here on Earth?" I asked Umba-Wumba.

The alien jumped up and down. He was happy and excited.

"I was at school yesterday," Umba-Wumba said, "and my teacher gave me some home-work. We had to write about another planet. I wanted to write about your planet –

Earth! So I borrowed my mother's space-time ship and came here."

Millie looked at Umba-Wumba. "You borrowed it?" she said.

Umba-Wumba waved his four hands. "Well, I took it, really. But I will get it back before my mother sees that it's gone."

I said, "Umba-Wumba! But what if she finds out? Your mother will be so angry with you."

Umba-Wumba waved his nose. "But I wanted to see you again and write all about Earth for my home-work."

I put my finger on my chin and began to think. "Mmm ..." I said.

Millie looked at me. "What?"

"I have a good idea," I said.

Millie groaned. "Oh, no! I don't like your ideas. They always get us into danger!"

Umba-Wumba said, "What's your good idea?"

I looked at my orange friend. "You could take us in your space-time ship," I said. "We could go back in time and have an adventure!"

Millie said, "Oh, no, Mouse!"

"Why not?" I said.

I told Umba-Wumba about the home-work we had to do, all about dinosaurs.

"We could go back in time to see the dinosaurs," I said. "Then you can do your home-work about planet Earth, Umba-Wumba. And we can find out all about dinosaurs."

Umba-Wumba jumped up and down like a big ball. "Yes! What a great idea!"

But Millie shook her head. "No! It's a silly idea. What if we got lost, or something went wrong?"

I said, "But it will be a fun way to learn about dinosaurs, Millie."

Umba-Wumba held Millie's hand. "Please come with us, Millie. We'll have a great time in the past! And I'll bring us back safely. Your mum and dad won't even know you've been away."

"Please, Millie!" I said.

"Come with us!" Umba-Wumba said.

At last Millie nodded. "OK, I'll come," she said. "You two might get into danger. You'll need me to look after you!"

We held hands and ran into the space-time ship.

# Chapter 3
# Into the Past

"Sit down and hold on tight," Umba-Wumba told us. "This will be very bumpy."

We sat in the seats. Umba-Wumba stood at the controls and hit a lot of buttons with his four hands.

Seconds later the ship began to shake like a washing machine. My teeth rattled. I looked at Millie. She smiled bravely.

I looked out of the window. I could see grass, and trees, and some cows eating the grass.

Then the cows and the grass vanished. Now it was dark outside the window.

Umba-Wumba held onto the controls and said, "We're moving back in time. Look."

He pointed to a screen on the wall. The screen showed some numbers. They were moving very fast: 2009, 2000, 1990, 1980...

Millie said, "That's the date, Mouse! We're going back in time!"

I looked at the numbers. They were a blur. Soon it was 1950, and then 1900, and then 1800.

Soon the numbers were moving so fast that we couldn't see them. The ship still rattled, and a loud hum filled the room.

I closed my eyes and wished that we would soon arrive in the time of the dinosaurs.

"1500!" Umba-Wumba said. "500! Now it's 1000 BC ..."

The rattle got louder and louder. Millie gripped my hand and held on to it.

"Now we're five thousand years in the past ... and now ten thousand!" Umba-Wumba said.

I gripped Millie's hand. I felt sick.

"Fifty thousand years in the past!" Umba-Wumba yelled. "One hundred thousand years in the past!"

Millie said, "I hope we get there soon. My tummy feels a bit funny."

Umba-Wumba shouted, "Five hundred thousand years in the past. One million! Five million!"

Five million years in the past! What would it look like out there?

"Twenty million years in the past," Umba-Wumba said. "Seventy million years. One hundred and fifty million years. We're there!"

Suddenly the hum stopped. Then the rattle stopped. The trip was over.

We had gone back in time one hundred and fifty million years, to the time of the dinosaurs.

Millie looked out of the window. The green field and the cows were gone. All we could see was a jungle and tall trees.

"I don't see any dinosaurs," Millie said.

"Let's go out and see if we can find some," Umba-Wumba said.

He moved to the door and opened it. I held Millie's hand and we stood at the top of the ramp. Far away I could hear roars.

Millie looked at me. "I wonder if the roars are dinosaurs?"

Umba-Wumba bounced down the ramp, into the jungle. "Come on!" he shouted. "It's lovely and warm."

Slowly we walked down the ramp and looked around. I wondered if I would soon see a dinosaur.

We had landed in a jungle clearing between the tall trees. We followed Umba-Wumba away from the ship.

Umba-Wumba stopped. "Listen," he said.

We stood very still and listened.

I heard a sound. Something was crashing through the forest. I heard the swish of trees, and then a roar.

"GRAH-GRAH!"

"Quick!" Millie cried. She pulled me and Umba-Wumba behind a tree. We crouched down and looked out at the clearing.

"Look!" I said.

# Chapter 4
# Run For Your Life

A dinosaur stepped into the clearing.

I had seen dinosaurs in books and in films – but now I was looking at a dinosaur in real life.

"Look how big it is!" Millie said.

Another dinosaur joined the first one. They were big animals with very long necks and even longer tails. They were bigger than a bus and they moved very slowly.

"If they see us," I said, "then they'll eat us!"

Millie giggled. "You are silly, Mouse. These dinosaurs are called brachiosaurs. They eat plants. They don't eat meat. Look."

The two brachiosaurs stomped around the clearing and reached up to the tall trees with their long necks. They pulled leaves from the trees and chewed them. Then I saw two more dinosaurs. These were babies. They were much smaller than the huge brachiosaurs – but even the babies were as big as cars.

"They're ... lovely!" Millie said.

The babies rolled across the clearing. They nipped each other's tails and made small growls.

"It's a family," Millie said. "Mum and Dad and two cute babies."

I watched Mum and Dad eat the leaves. They swung their long necks from side to side and roared.

Millie opened her school bag and pulled out her home-work book.

"What are you doing?" I said.

She began to write in her home-work book. "I'm doing my home-work." She looked at the dinosaurs. "I'm making notes. Mr Brooke told us that no one knows what colour dinosaurs were. We only have fossils of their bones now. We're the first people to see real, live dinosaurs!"

The brachiosaurs were yellow, with big red spots dotted all over their bodies. "They look like they've jumped into a bath of jelly and custard!" I said.

Millie looked up from her home-work book. "Wait till we get back and tell Mr Brooke!"

Suddenly the brachiosaurs stopped eating. They stood very still and held their heads to one side, and listened to something.

"What's wrong?" I said.

Then Umba-Wumba jumped up and down. "Do you hear that?" he yelled. "Listen!"

Something moved in the jungle, very close to us. We knelt down behind the tree trunk. I looked all around, but I didn't see any dinosaurs.

"Gubble!" Umba-Wumba cried. "Look!"

The brachiosaurs were moving away from the clearing as fast as they could move their big bodies. The babies went first, running fast.

Then I heard something crash through the jungle.

Four more dinosaurs jumped into the clearing. They were smaller than the brachiosaurs – but they were still much bigger than Millie and me. They stood up on two feet and ran quickly. They chased the brachiosaurs and roared. I was happy that the baby brachiosaurs had got away.

"GRAAH!" the new dinosaurs cried.

"But the brachiosaurs are much bigger," I said. "Why are they running away?"

Millie said, "The brachiosaurs are plant-eaters, Mouse. And these new dinosaurs ... I think they are called allosaurs. They eat meat!"

We watched the four allosaurs run after the brachiosaurs. The allosaurs were even more colourful than the bigger dinosaurs.

They had green and yellow stripes on their bodies.

"They look like they have football shirts on!" I said.

Then the allosaurs attacked the brachiosaurs. The clearing was filled with roars and growls. I closed my eyes. I didn't want to see the big, peaceful brachiosaurs get eaten by the allosaurs.

Umba-Wumba said, "That's funny. I wonder why the allosaurs have stopped chasing the brachiosaurs?"

I opened my eyes and looked across the clearing.

"Because they've seen the space-time ship!" I said.

The allosaurs were moving around Umba-Wumba's ship. They looked into the window.

One allosaur walked up the ramp and looked through the window in the door.

Umba-Wumba gripped my arm. "Look!"

He pointed to the ship with one of his four arms. The allosaur was moving away from the ship's door. It came our way and sniffed the air with its long nose.

"But how did it know we are here?" Millie said.

"Maybe it can smell us," I said. "Mr Brooke told us they have a great sense of smell."

"And it's a meat-eater!" Millie said.

I didn't want to be dinosaur food!

"Run!" Umba-Wumba cried. We ran.

The problem was, the allosaur wasn't big and slow. It was fast …

# Chapter 5
## Escape

We ran for our lives. Umba-Wumba bounced along like a ball.

The allosaur roared and crashed through the trees. For a small dinosaur, it had a very loud roar.

What would it be like to be eaten by a dinosaur? What would Mum and Dad say when I didn't come home?

I looked behind us. The green and yellow allosaur was closer to us now. It had a pointed head, with a long snout and a lot of sharp teeth.

It looked hungry. It roared as it ran after us. "GRAAH!"

I almost fell over, but Millie held onto my hand and pulled me along after her. She looked over her shoulder. "Oh, no!"

"What?" I cried.

"Now all four allosaurs are running after us!"

They crashed through the jungle and roared. They sounded very angry – and hungry as well.

"This way!" Umba-Wumba said.

We were going downhill now. I could hear the allosaurs roar at us. They were getting closer every second. We came to a big drop.

"Jump!" Umba-Wumba said.

I closed my eyes and jumped.

We were flying in the air. I opened my eyes and yelled.

We hit the ground and rolled.

I bumped my head and yelled. I sat up and looked for Millie and Umba-Wumba. Millie sat near me. She rubbed her arm.

"Are you OK, Millie?"

"I just banged my arm, Mouse. I'll be fine." She looked round. "Where is Umba-Wumba?"

We couldn't see our orange friend.

"Umba-Wumba!" we called, but he didn't call back.

We could see the green and yellow allosaurs at the top of the hill. We ran behind a bush and hid. The allosaurs looked down the hill, but they couldn't see us.

Soon the allosaurs moved away. We were safe, for a little while.

"Now," Millie said, "where is Umba-Wumba?"

# Chapter 6
# Where is Umba-Wumba?

I called out, "Umba-Wumba, where are you?"

Millie said, "Perhaps he hit his head when he fell, and knocked himself out."

Umba-Wumba was mostly all one big head – so he had a lot of head to hit. "I hope not," I said.

"But where can he be?" asked Millie.

I said, "Maybe Umba-Wumba rolled when he hit the ground. Maybe he's down there in the long grass?"

"Come on," Millie said. "Let's go and look for him."

We set off. I found a stick and hit the grass and leaves in front of us.

"Umba-Wumba!" Millie called.

"If we don't find him," I said, "how will we get back home? Even if we did get back into the ship, we don't know how to make it work."

We came to a river. "Perhaps," I said, "he fell into the water and was swept away?"

"Or maybe," Millie said, "he fell into the river and drowned."

I looked in the water for his little round body, but I couldn't see him.

Millie called out, "Look!"

"Oh, no," I said.

A huge dinosaur stood near the river. It held something in its arms.

It was holding Umba-Wumba. Our little orange friend was all floppy. I wondered if he was dead.

The dinosaur saw us. It waved an arm at us – then it roared. It didn't sound like the other dinosaurs.

The dinosaur moved towards us, slowly at first. Then it began to run. It yelled at us. It sounded like a low rumble.

Millie grabbed my hand. "Run!" she cried.

We raced through the jungle and jumped over fallen trees. I looked back. The dinosaur was still chasing us. It held Umba-Wumba in one arm and waved at us with the other arm.

Seconds later we jumped behind a big tree and hid.

I took a peek round the tree. The dinosaur was looking for us. It was making funny sounds.

"That's the oddest dinosaur I've ever seen," Millie said. "I mean, the way it speaks. And have you noticed, Mouse – it's wearing a silver coat."

I looked around the tree again. Millie was right. The dinosaur wore a silver coat.

"But what does it want with Umba-Wumba?" I said. "Is it a meat-eater?"

"I don't know," Millie said. "I've never seen a dinosaur like this one."

The dinosaur put Umba-Wumba on the ground. Our orange friend didn't move. Was he still alive? Maybe the fall down the hill had killed him?

I didn't like to think about that.

"Oh, Mouse," Millie said. "Look."

The dinosaur had put Umba-Wumba down next to a big pile of fruit. Now the dinosaur sat down and picked up a fruit with its claws and ate it.

"Oh, no," Millie said. "It thinks Umba-Wumba is a bit of fruit. It's going to eat him!"

# Chapter 7
# The Plan

"What can we do to save Umba-Wumba?" I said.

"I have an idea," Millie said. "We've got to get the dinosaur away from Umba-Wumba."

"Yes, but how can we do that?"

"Easy," Millie said. "I'll run into the clearing, and then I'll run away and the dinosaur will run after me. Then you can save Umba-Wumba."

"But what if the dinosaur gets you?" I said.

Millie smiled. "It won't, Mouse. I'm a fast runner, even faster than you. I'll meet you back at this tree in two minutes, OK?"

"Millie, don't do it!" I said.

"But I've got to," Millie said. "I've got to save Umba-Wumba!"

I gave Millie a hug. She looked into the clearing, at the dinosaur in the silver coat. It ate some fruit and said something to Umba-Wumba.

But Umba-Wumba lay very still, and the eye on the end of his nose was shut.

Millie smiled at me. "Here I go," she said.

She ran into the clearing. She stood in front of the dinosaur and danced up and down and waved her arms. The dinosaur looked up and saw her.

Millie ran into the jungle. The dinosaur looked hard at her. Then it ran after her. Soon the dinosaur vanished into the jungle after Millie.

I ran into the clearing. Umba-Wumba lay near the pile of fruit.

"Umba-Wumba!" I said. I put my hand on his big, round body.

Umba-Wumba groaned. He was still alive!

"Umba-Wumba!" I said. "We've got to get away from here. The dinosaur will be back soon."

Umba-Wumba opened the eye at the end of his nose.

"I fell down the hill," he said. "I bumped my head about ten times!"

"Then a dinosaur picked you up and carried you here," I told him. "It was going to eat you. But Millie ran into the clearing and the dinosaur went after her. Come on, let's go!"

I held his hand and we ran away. We hid behind the tree and sat down.

"I hope the dinosaur didn't get Millie," Umba-Wumba said.

"Millie can run fast," I told him. "She'll be here soon."

"And then we'll go back to the ship."

"But the allosaurs will still be there," I said. "What can we do?"

Umba-Wumba said, "Shh! I can hear something."

A loud crash and bang came from behind us. We looked back and saw two big legs stomp down near us.

It was the dinosaur!

Umba-Wumba dived to the ground. I jumped out of the way of the dinosaur's big feet.

The dinosaur moved past us and walked into the clearing.

"Oh, no!" Umba-Wumba said. "Look, it's got Millie!"

The dinosaur held Millie in its claws and looked at her.

The dinosaur sat down in the clearing near the fruit. But it didn't put Millie down. It held her up, near its face.

"I think it's going to eat her!" I said.

# Chapter 8
# The Lonely Alien

The dinosaur opened its mouth.

I closed my eyes. I didn't want to see the dinosaur eat my best friend.

Then Umba-Wumba began to laugh.

I opened my eyes and looked at him. "What's so funny?"

My orange friend pointed into the clearing. "Look," he said.

The dinosaur still held Millie, but it didn't eat her. The dinosaur talked to her. Millie nodded her head and talked to the dinosaur.

Millie looked up and called out to us, "Mouse! Umba-Wumba! It's OK. Come here!"

She waved to us and the dinosaur put Millie down on the ground.

I walked into the clearing with Umba-Wumba. We looked at Millie and the dinosaur. "We were afraid it was going to eat you," Umba-Wumba said.

The dinosaur looked down at us with eyes as big as footballs. Then it smiled at us.

Millie looked very happy. "Meet Gur," she said. "Gur, meet my friends, Mouse and Umba-Wumba."

Then the dinosaur said, "I am very happy to meet you, Mouse and Umba-Wumba."

"You can speak English!" I said. "But how? You're a dinosaur!"

Millie giggled. "I felt it was odd that a dinosaur wore a silver coat, and I was right."

Gur said, "I'm not a dinosaur. I'm a Gando. I come from a planet called Gandon. I was in my space-ship, but it went wrong. I crashed and couldn't get my space-ship to work again. I've been here, all alone, for five years."

"Five years!" I said.

"And all the time I have dreamed of getting away from here," Gur said sadly.

Umba-Wumba waved his four arms and said, "Don't be sad any more, Gur. I think we can help you."

Gur looked at the little round alien. "You can? But how?"

"My space-time ship is in the jungle," Umba-Wumba said. "If we can get back to it, and get inside, then we can get away from here. I'll take Mouse and Millie back to their own time, and then I will take you to your planet."

"You can do that?" Gur said. He smiled and showed all his big teeth. "Oh, I really want to get away from this place! I don't like dinosaurs. All they do all day is roar and eat each other! I've been so lonely here."

"But the allosaurs are all round the space-time ship," Millie said. "We can't go back or the allosaurs will attack us."

Gur said, "I think I can help you. We'll go back to your ship, and I will run after the allosaurs and chase them away. Then you can

49

get into the ship. I'll jump in after you and then we can get away."

"Good idea," Umba-Wumba said.

Gur said, "Now get onto my back. It will be quicker if I give you a ride to the ship."

I stepped onto Gur's tail. "Ow," he said. "Perhaps you should take off your shoes, Mouse and Millie."

I took off my shoes.

"Pooh!" Millie said. "Your socks stink!"

"They're my football socks," I said. "I didn't take them off after games today."

"Well, take your socks off and put them in your school bag!" Millie told me.

I pulled off my stinky socks and put them in my bag. Then I jumped onto Gur's tail and climbed up and up and up – it was like walking up a very long stair-case. I sat down on his back and held Millie's hand. Umba-Wumba came next and sat beside us. Gur stood up and began to walk.

I held onto Gur's back as we swung from side to side. We were very high up, above all the tree-tops. It was like going on a fair-ground ride.

"Hold on tight!" I said. "We don't want to fall all the way down to the ground."

Gur tramped along. He stomped on plants and knocked trees down.

Two minutes later Millie said, "Look, I can see the space-time ship."

"And the allosaurs are still there!" Umba-Wumba said.

# Chapter 9
# Into the Ship

Gur stopped behind some trees and we climbed down from his back. We hid behind a tree. I looked across the clearing. Four allosaurs moved round the ship, peering in the window.

Gur said, "Now I will chase the allosaurs away. Get ready to run into the ship, OK?"

We nodded. My heart was beating fast. What if I tripped up when I ran to the ship?

What if a meat-eating allosaur caught me and ate me?

"Here I go!" said Gur.

He ran towards the ship. He roared and waved his head from side to side, and showed his big teeth. "GRRR!"

Millie said, "He looks scary!"

The allosaurs all round the ship looked up. Gur was much bigger than the allosaurs, but there were four allosaurs and only one Gur! Seconds later Gur and two allosaurs were fighting. They rolled over and over on the ground and bit each other.

The other two allosaurs stood and watched the fight.

Umba-Wumba said, "Come on, let's go!"

I held Millie's hand and we ran. Umba-Wumba went first. He bounced along like a big orange ball.

"I hope Gur doesn't get hurt!" Millie shouted.

Gur was still fighting with the two allosaurs. He bit one of them on its tail and it screamed in pain and ran off into the jungle. Now Gur was fighting with just one allosaur. They rolled over and hit the ground with their bodies. The ground shook and Gur roared.

We were near the ship when I heard another loud roar.

I looked behind me. An allosaur had seen us and was running after us. It roared. I thought it was saying, "Yes, you three will make a very nice meal, thank you!"

I cried out and ran faster.

Millie said, "It's getting closer!"

I had an idea. As I ran, I opened my school bag.

"What are you doing?" Millie yelled.

The allosaur roared again. It was right behind us. "GRAAH!"

I pulled my stinky socks from my school bag. "Mr Brooke said that meat-eating dinosaurs had a great sense of smell. Well, this might stop the allosaur!"

I threw my socks over my shoulder.

Suddenly the allosaur stopped roaring.

I looked back as I ran. The allosaur was not coming after us. It had stopped running and was looking hard at the ground. It bent down and sniffed my socks. Then it opened its mouth and licked them up with its big tongue and started to eat them.

"Yuk! I said.

"Saved by your stinky socks!" Millie said.

Umba-Wumba got to the ship and ran inside. Seconds later we jumped into the ship. Umba-Wumba moved to the controls and we looked out of the window.

Outside, Gur stood up and ran away from the allosaur.

"Hurry up!" Millie yelled.

Gur ran up the ramp and jumped into the ship. He was big, and the ship was small, but he pushed himself into the control room. It was a tight fit, with all four of us in the room. I was pressed up between Gur's green belly and Umba-Wumba's orange body.

Outside the window, I saw the allosaur. It still chomped on my socks. It looked up, then ran to the ship and looked into the window.

"I think it wants more smelly socks!" Millie said.

The allosaur was about to smash the glass and poke its claw at us.

Then Umba-Wumba pressed a button. The ship began to rattle and the allosaur vanished.

We were on our way home!

# Chapter 10
# Off to Bed

Soon the screen on the wall showed the date: 2000, then 2005, and then 2009.

The space-time ship slowed down and the engine noise stopped. We looked out of the window. We could see green fields and trees and a cow munching grass.

"We're home!" Millie yelled.

"And now I'll take Gur back to the planet Gandon," Umba-Wumba said.

"Thank you so much, Umba-Wumba," Gur said.

Millie hugged Umba-Wumba, and then I hugged him. "It was great to see you again, Umba-Wumba."

"I'll come back again one day, and we'll go on another adventure!"

"But next time," Millie said, "please don't take us to see any dinosaurs!"

We said good-bye to Gur, and thanked him for helping us. Then we left the ship. We turned and waved to Umba-Wumba and Gur as the ship took off, flying high into the sky.

"Good-bye, Umba-Wumba," Millie said.

We walked home.

"Do you still think dinosaurs are boring, Mouse?"

"Not boring – just scary," I said. "And Mr Brooke was right. Meat-eating dinosaurs do have a great sense of smell! I'm glad I remembered that."

"So you see, Mouse – some facts are interesting, and useful!"

I smiled. "I wonder if the allosaur liked the taste of my smelly socks?"

When we got to my house, I said good-bye to Millie and went inside.

Mum and Dad were in the kitchen.

Mum looked at me. Her mouth fell open. "Mouse!" she said. "Where on earth have you been? There is mud all over you! And your feet! What have you done with your socks?"

"Oh," I said. I looked down at my bare feet. "Well, you see ... It's a long story. But a dinosaur ate my socks!"

"That's the silliest excuse I ever heard, Mouse!" Dad said. "Off to bed!"

I went up to my room and lay on my bed. I smiled and took my home-work book from my school-bag.

Then I wrote all about our adventures with the dinosaurs.

*******

At school on Monday, Mr Brooke said, "Now, class, I've read all your home-work about dinosaurs. I liked your story, Mouse. In fact, I liked it so much that you can read it out."

I stood up in front of the class.

I could see Millie. She put a hand over her mouth and giggled.

I opened my home-work book and began to read.

All the boys and girls, and Mr Brooke, were thinking I had made up the story. But Millie and I knew that it had really happened – and Umba-Wumba and Gur did too.

"A Dinosaur Ate My Socks," I said. "I was walking home from school with my best friend Millie ..."

Barrington Stoke would like to thank all its readers for commenting on the manuscript before publication and in particular:

Felix Allan

Will Baker

Fiona Devereux

Sam Egerton

Praise Gwasira

Janine Hickman

Oliver Kemp

Mikey Kingston

Alexander Kyle

Konrad Lbyrowski

Luke McShane

Ben Morris

Pam Reid

Philippa Ann Watson

Marcus Watt

## Become a Consultant!

Would you like to give us feedback on our titles before they are published? Contact us at the email address below – we'd love to hear from you!

info@barringtonstoke.co.uk
www.barringtonstoke.co.uk